This book belongs to

casey   chloe

Five-minute FAIRY —Tales—

p

CONTENTS

The Clumsy FAIRY

Did you know that all fairies have to go to school to learn *how* to be fairies? Well they do! They have to learn how to fly, how to be graceful and how to do magic. Some fairies find it difficult. Clementine did!

Poor Clementine. She was the worst in the class. She was clumsy and awkward. When they were dancing she was the only fairy who tripped over her own feet.

"Clementine! Think of feathers, not elephants,"

Madame Bouquet, the fairy dance teacher, was forever saying.

At the end of term all the fairies were given a special task for the holidays. Sweetpea and Beatrice had to make garlands of flowers for the May Ball. Jemima and Poppy had to collect honey from the bees. Breeze and Scarlet had to polish the leaves on the holly tree.

But there was one task that no one wanted. This was to help a little girl who had measles.

"Clementine," said Madame Bouquet, "I want you to take this rose petal lotion, and paint it on the little girl's spots when she is asleep," said Madame Bouquet. "If you do this every night, for one whole week, the spots will disappear."

Clementine couldn't wait to start. That night she flew to the little girl's house and in through the bedroom window. So far so good! The little girl's name was Alice, and Clementine could see her fast asleep in bed. She was holding a fat, round teddy in her arms.

Clementine crept towards the bed. Then she tripped over the rug and sat on a prickly hairbrush which was lying on the floor.

"Ouch!" she yelled.

Alice stirred, but didn't wake. Clementine got up quietly. She bent over to pick up the hairbrush, and a toy clown, with a silly face, pinched her bottom!

"Ouch!" she yelled again.

This time Alice did wake up. "Who's there?" she asked sleepily.

"It's Clementine," said the fairy, "and your clown just pinched my bottom!"

"Never did!" said the clown.

"Are you sure?" Alice asked Clementine, rubbing her eyes. "He's usually very well behaved."

Then Clementine overbalanced and sat down quickly on Alice's hot-water bottle which was lying on the floor. It was so bouncy that she shot straight up in the air and landed with a plop on Alice's bed.

"Are you alright?" asked Alice, rubbing her eyes again to make sure she wasn't seeing things.

Clementine smoothed her crumpled dress and fluttered her wings. She explained to Alice why she had come.

"I'm sorry I woke you," she added. "You're not really supposed to see me."

Alice didn't mind. She thought it was lovely to be able to talk to a real fairy.

"Can you really do magic?" she asked Clementine.

"Yes," Clementine told her. "I'm quite good at magic. I just wish I wasn't so clumsy."

She told Alice about her dance classes and Alice told Clementine about her ballet lessons.

"If you are helping me get rid of my measles," she said to Clementine, "I'll help you with your ballet."

So each night Clementine went to see Alice. Alice taught Clementine how to point her toes, how to keep her balance on one foot and how to curtsy gracefully. Clementine worked hard to copy everything Alice showed her. But it was the pirouette that Clementine did best of all. Holding her arms high above her head she twirled and twirled round Alice's bedroom.

In return, Clementine painted Alice's spots. Each day they became fainter and fainter. By the end of the week they had gone.

After the holidays the fairies went back to school.

"Now fairies," said Madame Bouquet, "I want you to show me *The Dance of the Sugar Plum Fairy.*"

The music started and the fairies began to dance. And, do you know, Clementine was the best dancer in the class. Madame Bouquet couldn't believe her eyes.

"Why, Clementine," she gasped, "you're my prima ballerina!"

And 'prima', as I'm sure you know, means 'first and best'!

Clementine was the happiest fairy in the world!

Misery the GRUMPY — Fairy —

Misery didn't have any friends. It was her own fault–she was always grumbling. She grumbled at the fairy who baked the bread. She grumbled at the fairy who mended her shoes. She even grumbled at the fairy who collected her honey. Willow, her niece, couldn't understand her.

"Why do you always find fault with everyone?" she asked.

"Because everybody is so useless," said her grumpy aunt.

One day Misery told the
fairy who baked the bread,
"Your bread is too soft. I
like crusty bread."

"If that's your attitude,"
said the baker fairy, "you
can bake your own bread."

"I shall!" said Misery.

The next day she was rude to the
fairy who mended her shoes.

"No one speaks to me like that!" said the cobbler
fairy. "From now on you can
mend your own shoes."

"I'll be glad to," said
Misery grumpily.

Then she insulted the
fairy who collected the
honey from the honeybees.

"How dare you?" said the
fairy. "I'm not staying here to be

insulted. You can collect your own honey." And she stormed off.

Soon there was no one in the village who would do anything for Misery.

"You've been rude to everyone," said Willow. "How are you going to manage?"

"No problem," said Misery. "I shall do everything myself."

She set to work the very next day to bake some bread. First she lit a fire to get the oven really hot. Then she made some dough and mixed and kneaded it until her arms ached. Then she left the dough to

rise. She put the loaf in the oven, and sat down for a well-earned rest.

Of course, she fell asleep! A smell of burning woke her! Rushing to the oven she flung open the door. All that was left of the loaf of bread were a few burnt cinders.

But what Misery didn't realise was that the baker fairy didn't bake bread in the usual way. No! She used a special baking spell – a spell that Misery didn't know!

Misery was still determined to carry on. She went to collect some honey from the bees. She watched them buzzing round the hive. Misery just waved her arms at them, shouting, "Out of my way, bees."

They didn't like it one little bit!

Their answer was to swarm around her and sting her nose and chin. You see, what Misery didn't know was that the honey fairy used the special honey-collecting spell.

Misery ran from the bees as fast as she could and, as she did, she lost her shoe!

Oh dear! What a state she was in! Burnt bread, bee stings on her nose and chin, and only one shoe!

"You can't go on like this," said Willow, when she saw her.

Misery did some serious thinking.

"Tell all the fairies I've turned over a new leaf," she told Willow. "From now on I shan't be a grumpy fairy any more."

Willow was delighted! So were the other fairies. Misery threw a large party as a way of saying sorry. Misery didn't complain about anything for months after that, and Willow kept her fingers crossed that it would last!

Sugarplum
- and the -
BUTTERFLY

"Sugarplum," said the Fairy Queen, "I've got a very important job for you to do."

Sugarplum was always given the most important work. The Fairy Queen said it was because she was the kindest and most helpful of all the fairies.

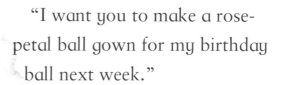

"I want you to make a rose-petal ball gown for my birthday ball next week."

"It will be my pleasure," said Sugarplum happily. She liked being busy.

She set to work straight away. Sugarplum began to gather cobwebs to make the thread, and rose petals to make the dress. While she was collecting the thread she found a butterfly caught in a cobweb.

"Oh, you poor thing," sighed Sugarplum. She stopped what she was doing to help him. Very carefully, Sugarplum untangled the butterfly. But his wing was broken. Sugarplum laid the butterfly on a bed of feathers.

He was very sick and weak with hunger. Sugarplum gathered some nectar from a special flower and fed him a drop at a time. Then she set about mending his wing with a magic spell. Every day Sugarplum fed the butterfly with nectar and cast her spell to mend his wing. After six days, the butterfly was better. He was very grateful. But by now Sugarplum was behind with her work!

"I shall never finish the Fairy Queen's ball gown by tomorrow," she cried. "Whatever shall I do?"

The butterfly comforted her.

"Don't worry, Sugarplum," he said. "We will help you." He gathered all his friends together. There were yellow butterflies, blue butterflies, red and brown butterflies. He told them how Sugarplum had rescued him from the cobweb and helped to mend his wing. The butterflies gladly gathered up lots of rose petals and dropped them next to Sugarplum. Then the butterflies flew away to gather more cobwebs, while Sugarplum arranged all the petals.

Back and forth went Sugarplum's hand with her needle and thread making the finest cobweb stitches. Sugarplum added satin ribbons and bows. When she had finished, Sugarplum was very pleased.

"Dear friend," she said to the butterfly, "I couldn't have finished the dress without your help."

"And I couldn't have flown again without your kindness," said the butterfly.

The Fairy Queen was delighted with her new ball gown. And, when she heard the butterfly's story, she wrote a special 'Thank You' poem for Sugarplum:

Sugarplum is helpful,
Sugarplum is kind.
Sugarplum works hard all day,
But she doesn't mind.
She always does her very best,
To make sick creatures well.
She brings such joy and pleasure
As she weaves her magic spell!

The FOOTBALL Fairy

Georgina loved to play football. But there was just one problem.

"I'm fed up with these silly wings," she said, wiggling her shoulders. "They just get in the way."

The other fairies didn't agree at all.

"Whoever heard of a fairy without wings?" laughed Twinkletoes, doing a little dance.

"You wouldn't be able to fly if you didn't have wings," said Petal, landing on a flower.

"Flying is brilliant," called Sparkle, sprinkling fairy dust.

"Keep that fairy dust away from me," sneezed Georgina crossly. "I'm going to play football."

"Football is a game for elves, not fairies!" said Sparkle.

"In that case, I don't want to be a fairy!" said Georgina, and stamped off.

"She'll change her mind," said the wise fairy, "just wait and see."

But Georgina wouldn't change her mind. She pulled on her football boots and went to play with the elves.

The football game was very rough. The ball bounced around the field and, quite often, off the field! Sometimes it went up into the trees. Two birds who were trying to build their nest got very fed up, especially when the football landed near them.

Georgina flew up to get it. "Perhaps my wings can be useful after all," she thought, landing on the ground. She looked round quickly, hoping no one had seen her.

But someone had! Barry, the elf, was a tell-tale! He couldn't wait to tell the fairies what he had seen.

"Ah," nodded the wise fairy. "I knew she would use her wings sooner or later." But Georgina still wouldn't join in with the other fairies.

The next time she played football, the game was

rougher than ever. One elf
kicked the ball so hard it
flew into the tree and hit
the birds' nest. This time
there was an egg in it! The
egg began to topple. None
of the elves noticed; they were
far too busy arguing with the
referee. So Georgina flew up and,
just in time, caught the egg before it hit
the ground. Then she flew up to the nest.

"Thank you," said the
mummy bird, rather
sternly, tucking the egg
back under her. "But
please, in future, be
more careful when
you play football!"

Georgina promised
she would.

When she flew down from the tree, Barry the tell-tale elf saw her. Of course, he told the fairies. They looked knowingly towards Georgina. "What did I tell you?" said the wise fairy. "She'll soon come round to being one of us."

Next time she played football, Georgina checked the tree first. The mummy bird was away. "Good!" she thought. "She can't complain this time." But, thanks to a naughty elf, the football knocked into the birds' nest. A small bundle of feathers tumbled out. It was a baby bird!

Georgina spotted it and, quick as lightning, she flew up to catch him. Gently, she held him in her arms and flew back to the nest. When he was safely inside she sprinkled him with fairy dust to keep him from further harm. Just then mummy bird came back.

"I shall tell everyone about your kindness," she said, as her baby snuggled under her feathers. "And, as you're such a good fairy, will you be baby Beak's godmother?"

"I'd be delighted!" said Georgina.

When they heard the news, the other fairies were very proud of her.

"Perhaps it's not so bad being a fairy after all," grinned Georgina.

- The Tooth -
FAIRY

Pansy was nearly five. She couldn't wait for her birthday because Mum had promised her a party in the garden. There would be birthday cake and balloons and a funny clown. All her friends were coming to her party.

There was only one problem! Pansy's two front teeth were loose. They wobbled whenever she bit into anything. How was she going to enjoy her party food?

"Mum," she asked, for the

hundredth time, "will my wobbly teeth come out before my birthday party?"

"They'll come out when they're ready," said Mum, smiling.

That night Pansy woke suddenly. The curtains were open and her bed was covered in silvery moonlight. But that wasn't all! Sitting on Pansy's pillow was … can you guess? A fairy! It's true! She was tiny, with pale yellow wings, a wand and a sparkly dress.

Pansy could hardly believe it. She stared at the fairy, and the fairy stared back at her. The fairy spoke first.

"Can you see me?" she asked.

"Yes," said Pansy.

"That's funny," said the little fairy. "Usually I'm invisible!"

"Are you the tooth fairy?" asked Pansy.

"Yes, I'm Bobo," said the fairy. "I need two tiny front teeth to replace the keys on my piano."

Pansy showed Bobo her two front teeth. They were *very* wobbly.

"I hope they come out before my birthday party," said Pansy.

"They'll come out when they are ready," said Bobo. "If they come out before your birthday, I'll play my piano at your party!"

The next day, Bobo peeped into the playroom and found Pansy standing on her head!

"What are you doing, Pansy?" she asked.

"If I stay like this all day," said Pansy, "my teeth might fall out."

At teatime Bobo watched from behind a bowl of fruit, as Pansy ate all her cheese on toast, including the crusts. But still her teeth didn't come out!

"Try brushing your teeth," Bobo whispered to her, before Pansy went to bed.

"Oh yes! That will do it!" said Pansy. And she brushed and brushed and brushed, but the wobbly teeth just stayed stubbornly in her mouth.

The day before Pansy's birthday her two front teeth came out! It didn't hurt one little bit.

"Look!" she said to Mum, pulling a face, and showing a big gap where her teeth should be.

"Scary! Scary!" laughed Mum, pretending to be frightened.

"These are for Bobo," said Pansy, showing Mum the teeth.

"Who's Bobo?" asked Mum.

"The tooth fairy, of course," said Pansy.

That night Pansy went to bed early. She put her teeth under the pillow.

"I'll just close my eyes for a minute," she said to herself, "but I won't go to sleep."

Later Bobo came in, but Pansy had already dozed off. Bobo even whispered Pansy's name, but Pansy was fast asleep.

Pansy didn't wake until the sun shone through her curtains the next morning. The first thing she did was look under the pillow. The two tiny teeth had gone! In their place were two coins.

Pansy's fifth birthday party was the best she'd *ever* had. All her friends came. There was jelly and ice cream, balloons and the funniest clown she'd ever seen.

Her friends sang 'Happy Birthday' so loudly that Mum had to put her fingers in her ears. But only *Pansy* could hear the tiny fairy playing a piano and singing 'Happy Birthday' in a silvery voice.

The Yellow
BLUEBELLs

The fairies at Corner Cottage were always busy. The garden was full of flowers and it was the fairies' job to look after them. You never saw them because they worked at night and hid during the day.

Blossom, the youngest fairy, was also one of

the busiest. It was her job to paint all the bluebells.

Corner Cottage had a lot of bluebells. They spread out under the apple tree like a deep, blue carpet.

One evening, Blossom was sick.

"I've got a terrible cold," she told her friend Petal, sniffing loudly. "I don't think I can work tonight."

"I wish I could help," said Petal, "but I've got to spray the flowers with perfume or they won't smell right. You'll have to ask the gnomes."

Oh dear! Nobody liked asking Chip and Chuck, the garden gnomes. All they liked doing was fishing and windsurfing on the pond and playing tricks. Blossom was very worried about asking them.

"No problem!" said Chip and Chuck when she asked them. "Just leave it to us."

But Blossom was right to worry! When she got up the next morning the gnomes had painted some of the bluebells ... YELLOW! She couldn't believe it.

"Have you seen what they've done?" she said to Petal. "What will Jamie think?"

Jamie lived in Corner Cottage with his mum and dad, and he played in the garden every day. That morning he came out as usual and made for the apple tree. It was a great tree for climbing. As he sat on his favourite branch, he looked down. Something looked different.

"I'm sure those flowers were blue yesterday," he thought.

"Mum," he said, going into the kitchen, "I've picked you some flowers."

"Yellowbells?" said Mum, putting them into a jam jar.

"Where did you get these?"

"Under the apple tree," said Jamie.

"How odd," said Mum. "I don't remember planting those."

That night, Blossom was still feeling ill.

"You'll have to paint the yellowbells again," she told the gnomes. But Chip and Chuck just chuckled.

In the morning, Jamie ran out to the garden and climbed the apple tree. This time the flowers were pink! He picked a bunch for his mum and she put them in the jam jar with the yellowbells.

When Petal told Blossom what had

happened, Blossom groaned. "I just knew something like this would happen." But she was still feeling too sick to work.

"Don't worry," said Petal. "Leave it to me." Petal made the naughty gnomes paint all the pinkbells again.

And this time she watched them carefully. The naughty gnomes grumbled loudly.

"Do it," said Petal, "or you'll never fish or windsurf on the pond again!"

The next morning, all the bluebells were blue again. Blossom was feeling much better.

"I'll be glad to get back to work!" she told Petal.

When Jamie and his mum went into the garden,

everything was as it should be. The bluebells were the right colour. And there was no sign of the yellowbells or pinkbells.

"It must have been the fairies!" joked Mum.

That night, as Jamie lay in bed he heard laughing and splashing from the fishpond. But, when Jamie peered through window, he couldn't see anything.

"Maybe it really was the fairies," he thought as he drifted off to sleep.

Written by Jan and Tony Payne, Likely Stories
Illustrated by Rory Tyger (Advocate)
Language consultant: Betty Root
Design by Design Principals

This is a Parragon Book
First published in 2002

Parragon
Queen Street House
4 Queen Street
Bath BA1 1HE, UK

Printed in Spain

ISBN 0-75258-590-8